ISBN-13: 979-8-9994578-5-1

Library of Congress Control Number: 2018675309
Printed in the United States of America

I0608521

This work is dedicated to all the free spirits, rebels, envelope-pushers, outcasts, and loners who pioneered their paths to success.

"First They Ignore You, Then They Laugh at You, Then They Attack You, Then You Win."

CONTENTS

"The Aggressor"

My wife and I spotted her across the dancefloor of the trendy honkytonk about the same that she spotted us over in the dark outskirts of the club. She wore brown cowgirl boots with jean shorts cut low enough to see the bottom quarter of her cheeks and a white spaghetti strap shirt tied into a knot in the front.

She flipped her white ranch hat up with a flick of the finger when she saw us. Hooking her thumbs in her belt straps, she danced over to us in an impressive side-step all the way across the dancefloor, darting between other dancers.

I felt Cindy tighten up beside me and her hand clinch my knee.

"Welllll, where have you been all night honey?" she asked Cindy.

"Right here people-watching," Cindy replied.

"I'm Kim," she said as she propped her elbows up on the tabletop and thrust her hips up and back for the world's consideration.

"Hi, Kim. I'm Cindy," Cindy said.

"Hi, Kim," I chimed in, noting that Kim was only staring at Cindy.

"I couldn't help but notice those big eyes while I was dancing out there, and I had to see who they belonged to," Kim said, biting her lower lip.

Cindy took a drink of her amaretto sour and I saw her grab for the pack of Marlboro Lights on the table, for a second forgetting she had to go outside to the patio to burn one. She quickly flinched her hand away, embarrassed.

"You two gonna buy me a drink or what?"

"Sure," I said, hailing a server.

The kid—probably a college kid—walked over when he noticed me but visibly mis-stepped when he saw Kim at the table.

"Whatch-whatcha havin'?" he stammered.

"Double shot of Jack, honey," Kim said.

"Ohh---okay." He took off without asking us.

Kim whistled at him. "Hey now, don't forget my new friends here. Bring them two double shots of Jack, too, bud."

"Sorry. Whoops. Sorry. You got it!"

"You dance here often?" Cindy asked.

"Oh, I dance here every night."

Cindy and Kim possessed some of the same attributes: Both had long, dark hair and big eyes. Both were busty and curvy, Cindy filling out her jeans and Kim filling out her shorts, stretching the limits of their clothes. But Kim was noticeably taller, somewhat hovering over Cindy, and stockier. Both were curvy in all the right places and trim in all the right places. The wingspan of Kim's ass noticeably exceeded her shoulders, but her tummy was flat and perfect. Cindy's tits were easily 34DD, but she had a petite figure otherwise, and when you looked at her, you could easily envision picking her up as she straddled you and taking her wherever you wanted.

"I'm gonna take your cherry, Cindy," Kim said as she pinched the cherry stalk and brought it upward, sticking out her long tongue to rim the cherry's bottom. Cindy started laughing, nervously, unsteadily. I felt her hand grasp my inner thigh, much tighter than previously.

"Well, no lady has taken that before. I've been holding out," Cindy said after a big gulp of the rest of her drink, her voice steadier now.

"You guys from out of town?" asked Kim.

"Yes, we live about an hour from here. We like to come down and have a date night every now and then," Cindy replied.

"Mmmm, okay," murmured Kim. "Where ya stayin'?"

"The Holiday Inn across the street," I said, adding, "We didn't want to drive."

"Well, walk me over there and let's talk about that cherry," she said and grabbed Cindy's hand before I even finished the sentence. Cindy looked back at me as we were heading out of the club, somewhat helplessly. I gave her a smug grin and followed, doing my best to keep up with the pair. Cindy stopped and lit a cigarette and Kim helped herself to one out of the pack and both smoked as they walked the few hundred yards across the parking lot and street to the hotel.

The clerk—another college kid, probably—stared at the ladies as they walked by and flashed a jealous frown. I shrugged, half-genuinely.

"Lord GAWD," I heard him say and looked back. His mouth was half-open with disbelief and coveting.

When we keyed the door to our first-room floor (right by the pool), Kim thrust Cindy against the wall in the hallway. I stood watching, unable to move around them. Kim pressed against Cindy, hard. Cindy threw her arms around Kim's neck as Kim rubbed her hands down Cindy's ass, squeezing. I heard a Cindy emit a tiny gasp.

Kim noticed me watching and threw her back in the direction of the bedroom. "Go sit down. This is girls' time."

My knees shaking, I slid around them, just barely able to squeeze through an opening, and fell back into the hotel chair.

Kim and Cindy made out in the hallway for a few minutes and ground up and down and against each other until Kim led

Cindy to the bed and pushed her down thereupon.

Kim fell on top of her. Cindy toyed with her ass, grasping one check with her left hand, and squeezing her lower cheek on the other side, winding her fingers quite easily into Kim's black, lace panties. Their asses facing me, I saw Cindy lightly petting and fingering Kim's pussy. Kim's pubic hair jutted out of her panties, the same color as the hair on top of her head. Kim shook her ass from side-to-side and Cindy began nibbling all over Kim's neck.

"Oh god, honey, you do that so good," Kim said.

"Stroke your cock while you watch us, baby," Cindy said to me as Kim jerked her shirt off Cindy's back as well as her black bra, exposing Cindy's ample breasts with large, round nipples. Kim took her tiny shirt off and pulled down her shorts and panties simultaneously. Kim pulled Cindy's blue jeans down and began grinding her face down in her cunt, licking all over her clit and fingering her pussy and ass unforgivingly.

Pre-cum had already slipped out of my cock as I began stroking slowly, savoring each moment. I edged myself out of climaxing repeatedly, seeing Cindy in a light I'd never before seen.

Kim's left nipple was pierced, and she had a dragon tattoo curved around her belly button. Cindy played with her tits as Kim went down on her, eating her pussy like she was dying of starvation.

Kim shook her ass at me and turned her head, the bottom of her chin glistening with Cindy's juices.

"None for you, bud. Don't you dare come out of that chair. Your wife's pussy belongs to me now."

My cock throbbed worse and worse with each uttered word.

Kim flipped around and positioned herself for a sixty-nine. Their tongues flicked on each other's pussies. Cindy moved her ass in a circular fashion as Kim fingered her pussy and licked her clit like it was an ice cream.

Cindy came suddenly, her moans muffled by Kim's muff grinding into her face. Kim did not relent, and flipped Cindy over as she came, down on her belly. Kim grasped her hips and shoved her up and back and continued going down on her. Her tongue licked all over her clit while her nose was buried in Cindy's pussy. She licked up and down, her tongue alternating from Cindy's ass to her pussy.

"Oh fuuuuu-fuuccckkkk," Cindy exclaimed. She could not control her movements and fell flat on her belly as she orgasmed.

Kim laid beside Cindy, plopping her nipple in her mouth as she caressed Cindy's body. Cindy licked and sucked on her nipple while she straddled Kim's thigh and pushed her pussy up on her. Cindy humped Kim's thigh as she hungrily sucked on Kim's nipple.

"Let's let him come over," Cindy said to Kim.

"Well, fine. I suppose. Come over here and stroke a little closer," Kim finally relented.

I laid beside Kim as the two kept humping each other. Kim rubbed her ass against me and then I felt Cindy's hand come across and began playing with my cock.

Kim half turned to watch Cindy stroke my cock.

"I'm going to own that cock now, too," Kim said as she mounted me and slid down on my cock all the way to my balls. I grunted and watched as she slowly rode me, her hands on my chest and my mouth on one of her nipples. Her breasts looked enormous as they hung.

Cindy relaxed on her arm and just observed. Her knees separated, and she fingered her clit as she watched Kim ride me.

"Oh, I fuckin' love this," said Cindy. "I love watching you fuck my husband."

"Oh, yeah," said Kim as she picked up speed. "Lick my pussy juice off his balls, baby."

Cindy did as she was told. I felt her lick all over my balls, sucking each one for good measure.

"Choke me, guy," Kim commanded.

I grabbed her throat and squeezed, slightly. She grabbed onto my hair and pulled hard.

"Squeeze harder. Do it."

I increased the pressure and Kim moaned with delight. Cindy positioned herself behind her, pressing her big tits against Kim's back as Kim's tits bounced up and down while she fucked me mercilessly.

"Don't you dare cum in me," she said. "But fuck me, fuck me, fuck me."

I squeezed her throat harder and grabbed onto her ass. I was on bottom but controlled her movements, thrusting my cock into her like it was a dagger. Each insertion caused Kim not to be able to fully catch her breath.

I felt her try to ease away from me but did not let her withdraw, making her big ass plop up and down and my cock without breaking a stride.

She kept pulling away, the sensation simply too much, until I felt her vaginal walls tighten and she came, her eyes rolling back in her head. She fell backwards into Cindy's arms, where Cindy played with Kim's nipples as I flooded Kim's pussy with my cum.

"Oh, you fucker—Oh, oh my god. My god! Fill me up. Fuck it. Fill this pussy up." I spanked her ass and came, completely inside her.

She fell off, trembling. Her legs involuntarily jerked.

Cindy smiled at me and climbed closer, cuddling me, and looking down at Kim at our feet, still semi-conscious.

"I own my wife's pussy, and I can own any pussy I want to," I told Kim as she slid off the bed and crawled to the bathroom, leaving a trail of cum from the bed to the bathroom.

KAY LACEY

"Rejuvenation"

The young blonde dressed in her cleaning scrubs sat at the kitchen table with her head down, buried in her cellphone. Roger's voice bellowed throughout the house:

"All I do is work, work, work. All the goddamn time. I spend eighty hours a week at the office and all you can apparently do is start failing businesses. You can't even keep a clean house. There's no reason you should have to hire somebody to help with this house."

From the corner of her eye, Gabby could discern Roger hovering over Sally in the den, who sat on the brown Italian leather couch, cowering. "Listen," she said, barely more than a whisper, "this is a big house. I just like some help every now and again. Gabby doesn't come every week. Just once a month. I just need a little help sometimes. I'm not as young as I used to be."

"Well, you can say that again," Roger laughed, deridingly. "Margot from school. That's who I should have married. She had flash, she had pizzazz. You know what? I settled. That's what I did. I bet Margot could run errands and clean the house and take care of the kids without this nonsense about being too busy. You're 45 years old and you haven't done anything with your life. Oh, poor you, poor you."

"But...but I supported you in school. I raised the kids and did everything while you worked. I feel like I've accomplished plenty," she said, her voice but a half-octave higher.

Gabby dared look up just for a moment. Roger was fit, although his beard and hair were graying. His back revealed no arch, and he stood straight as a fence post with his broad shoulders back. When Gabby saw him on prior occasions, he'd darted through the house like an athletic man in his twenties, unceasingly. He wore nice loafers and business or business casual clothes, always, steam-pressed, and perfect.

Sally, on the other hand, had mileage. Her dark brunette hair was constantly tussled. Gabby *only* saw her wear five-year-old yoga pants and t-shirts, her countenance in a perpetual "deer-in-the-headlights" gaze. She was a few pounds overweight, but her t-shirts could not hide her 34C breasts.

"I'm not listening to this. This is not a negotiation. These are facts. I support this family totally. I want you to get on the ball about the house, the kids, and your appearance. We have far too many public events for you to put in half-measures when it comes to your appearance. I have my reputation to uphold. I won't tolerate it. I need to always reflect success. At all times. Why would a client go to any attorney that didn't?"

"And you, Gabby," he said, walking the two steps up into the dining room and kitchen area, "don't get too comfortable. As soon as my wife figures out the facts of life, your services will no longer be needed. If I were you, I'd go to college instead of this menial stuff."

"I go to college. I do odd jobs to help with tuition."

"What? You don't have any parents to front your bills like every other damn Gen Z'er?"

"No. No parents. No student loans. I work."

He chuckled. "Look at that, Sally. That's called 'grit' right there. Maybe spend some time with this one so some of it may rub off."

He grabbed his briefcase from the kitchen island and stormed out, slamming the front door and peeling out in his Range Rover. When the screeching faded, Gabby discerned Sally's faint sobs in the den, where she held here head in her hands and wept like a grieving widow.

Gabby arose and walked to Sally, sitting beside her on the couch. The morning sun lit the room through the bay windows of the den, and the pool outside reflected brilliant hues into the home.

She put here arm around Sally. "I've got you. Just get it out."

"I...I just don't understand. I try to work and it's not good enough. I try to start a side business and he pulls the plug just when I get going. Nothing is ever just right for him. Never. He wants me here, but he wants me to contribute. I don't know what to do."

"I know. I know. I've been coming here six months and I've never seen you just lazing around. You contribute. He just doesn't want to see it. I hope I'm not over-stepping, but maybe it's time to consider whether you should stay in the marriage."

"What? I can't do that. We're Catholic. I just *can't*." She stared at Gabby with her eyes squinched, red, and puffy. Gabby's face contained some freckles here and there. Her eyes were piercing blue, and she maintained eye contact with Sally's dark brown irises.

"I'm not going to comment on your religion, but what I just saw was abusive. What I've seen here is abuse. Please think about it. I can't imagine what he does when a stranger isn't watching."

"Oh, it's horrible. He's just horrible."

Gabby held her closer, her perky breasts pressed up against Sally.

"Tell me something good. Tell me about a time you were happy."

Sally fell back against the couch and her sad eyelids drooped like a coon hound.

"The last time I was happy, I was in college. I was in theater. Back then, I was much more attractive. As a freshman, I was an understudy and stayed an understudy. I didn't mind. Theater was wild. There were very few egos. My friends and I just loved acting. We rehearsed until we couldn't anymore, and then we went to somebody's res hall or apartment and then we drank and smoked and had so much fun.

"It all felt so complete. This was before Roger. The world was my oyster. I was in total control of my fate. I fell in love hard during that time."

"Who did you fall in love with?"

Sally hesitated, and then confessed. "She was the star of our little troupe. Marilyn. She was voluptuous and carefree and such a brilliant actor. And she loved me, too. We would make love before class, after class. We'd make love and then rehearse our favorite scenes from movies.

"I'd never had an actual part in a performance until the last show of my senior year. Marilyn had already been accepted for her MFA and was going to California. She knew how I ached to be in a performance and she gave up her spot for me in *Death of a Salesman*. I was Laura Loman. For three shows, I was the center of campus, and I loved it, and I felt so alive. She did that for me."

Sally stared off into nothingness, ruminating on the memories with a faint smile, the tears drying.

"Life happened. We graduated. I went on to grad school. She went to Cali. That's where I met Roger. He was so precise and on top of everything in his life. He was so boring in school. But I knew he would never leave like she did, and I guess that's why we stayed together.

"I feel so powerless now. I'm so stuck. I don't think the kids even like me. I'm trapped in this life and in this house."

"I'm sure that's not true. No one is powerless. You just have to reclaim what you once had. There's a free spirit in there somewhere dying to get back out."

Sally focused on Gabby. "I suppose you're right," she smiled as she agreed. "I just don't know how to get back to what I was, but maybe I'll figure it out. Thank you for being so supportive when you come here."

Gabby winked at her. "It's my pleasure," she said as she put her head on Sally's shoulder and held her hand.

They sat in silence for a moment, Gabby caressing Sally's hand.

"You know...you actually look a lot like her."

"Like who? Marilyn?"

"Yes."

"Really?"

"Yes. In the face. I noticed it last time you were here. You're slenderer than her, but your face is a lot like hers. She'd kick my ass into shape if she were here. She was beautiful, but tough."

Gabby raised her head and looked at Sally. "I want you to listen to me. You're still in control of your life. You have power. You just have to find it."

"I'm afraid I just don't have anything left in me," Sally said.

"Look at me. Close your eyes and think about Marilyn. Think about that time in your life."

Sally complied, relaxing her head as Gabby began playing with her hair. "You're beautiful. You have such a nice body. You're vibrant. I've seen glimpses. Roger is lucky to have you. Marilyn was lucky to have you. I'm going to show you what kind of power you still have."

With that, Gabby mounted Sally, straddling her on the couch. Sally's eyes popped open.

"Gabby, what are you doing? We can't do this. You're half my age."

"I'm the same age as the love of your life was when you knew her. Pretend I'm her and pretend you're the past 'you.'"

Gabby left no time for protest, and locked lips with Sally, grinding her hips back and forth on her. Sally acquiesced, permitting her tongue to meet Gabby's with a little moan. Gabby broke at one point, sucking on Sally's tongue as she broke the embrace, and then attacked Sally's neck with soft, wet kisses.

Gabby discerned Sally squeezing her petite ass, faintly at first, and then squeezing like she was checking her cheeks to see if they were ripe. Gabby removed her blue scrub top, revealing perky tits with light, proportionate nipples. Freckles trickled down from her neck down into her bosom.

Gabby fell to her knees in the floor and tugged away at Sally's black yoga pants, pulling them down as Sally went ahead and slid her panties down. Gabby admired the pussy in front of her. Sally opened herself up to her, revealing a thick, dark bush and lips that spread open for Gabby, displaying a lengthy clit.

Gabby grasped Sally's hips and pulled her toward her, her lips locking with Sally's pussy, which was already gleaming with wetness. Gabby licked on Sally's clit horizontally, vertically, diagonally, made circles with her tongue. Sally removed her shirt and bra and stroked her tits, which were larger than Gabby's with large, dark areolas. Her nipples stood fully erect as she squeezed them.

"Oh yes, lick my pussy. Oh, God."

"Call me 'Marilyn.'"

"What? Really?"

"Yes."

"Okay. Lick my pussy, Marilyn. Lick it. Oh my god, I've missed you."

Gabby indulged herself with Sally's pussy for five minutes, with Sally responding to each flicker with a gasp, until Gabby ascended and began licking Sally's nipples. Gabby wrapped her legs around Sally as Gabby alternated licking each nipple.

Sally embraced one of Gabby's hands and thrust it down to her clit. Gabby aggressively and rhythmically rubbed her clit with authority. She picked up speed and kept licking Sally's nipples. Sally's body gyrated as she slowly geared to an orgasm.

"OHHHH FUUUUCCCKKKKKKK," Sally screamed as she gritted her teeth and half-moaned, half-growled as her bellows echoed throughout the large Cape Cod.

Overcome with the strength of the orgasm, Sally tried to push Gabby away, to no avail. Gabby restrained Sally with her weight and kept fingering her, making her orgasm fuller and longer. She only slowed as she felt Sally's orgasm waned.

"Now come here. Show me how powerful you are," Gabby commanded as she fell back on the rug in front of the fireplace and pulled down her bottoms, kicking off her Crocs. A narrow landing strip of blonde hair accentuated Gabby's young, tight pussy.

"Oh my, it's so beautiful," Sally said as she moved on all four to Gabby's pussy.

"Bend over," she told Gabby. "I want you like that."

Gabby quickly moved into the doggy position as Sally immediately began eating Gabby's asshole, her tongue darting in and out of her tiny opening.

"Oh....oh fuck, I wasn't expecting that. Oh shit," Gabby

commented as she held her weight up with one arm and began toying with her tiny clit as Sally's face buried itself in Gabby's ass and pussy, eating both in turn, over and over.

"Make me cum, baby. Do it. Fucking do it."

Sally grasped both Gabby's ass cheeks and began rocking her back-and-forth, holding out her tongue so that each time Gabby came back to her, her tongue penetrated her pussy. Sally kept penetrating her until she suddenly thrust Gabby back and inserted her tongue all the way into her pussy as far as it could go as she inserted her middle finger into Gabby's ass.

This combination coupled with her own rhythmic stroking of her clit caused Gabby to cum, seemingly from nowhere as Sally's knuckle disappeared in Gabby's ass.

Gabby made heaving movements as she came, falling to her elbows but leaving her ass straight up, constricting and contracting with each wave of her orgasm.

Sally fell back, exhausted, her tits jiggling as she hit the rug and Gabby's hips fell to one side. The pair fell silent, only their rapid breathing filling the room with any noise.

Slowly, Gabby crawled to beside Sally and cuddled with her. Sally turned on her side, with Gabby's tits pressed against Sally's ample ones, their legs locked, with pussy juice from both drenching each other.

"I love you, Marilyn," Sally said, stroking Gabby's blonde hair.

"I love you, Sally," she said as Sally began licking Gabby's tiny nipples. At the same time, both women began fingering each other, but this time slow and intimate. Sally licked her nipples until they began kissing again, playing with each other's tongue, exploring each other's clits.

Once more, as they were making out passionately and deeply, the two simultaneously orgasmed, Gabby breaking the kiss to press her face against Sally's neck, the two holding each other tightly as the orgasm peaked, and then valleyed.

They slept following this, locked with each other, each muzzled against the other.

When the moment finally gave way, Gabby put her clothes on weakly, kissing the sleeping Sally on her cheek before making her way to door. She silently closed the front door behind her, leaving her cleaning equipment in the foyer.

At one point, Sally awoke briefly and scanned the room. She found no one and made her way to the couch, cuddling up with a Vera Bradley throw blanket. She fell back asleep with a grin across her face.

Four hours later, Roger came home. He tossed his keys on the island along with his briefcase, popped a lager, and began walking to the den for a ballgame on the TV no doubt, when he discovered Sally on the couch.

"Sally! What the hell?"

"Hmmm???" she asked as she slowly opened her eyes and raised up, her squinted eyes honing in on Roger.

"Why are you asleep? It's dinner time, and this house looks shit. What happened to the cleaning girl? This is unacceptable. She's fired and you need to get up and take care of it."

Sally, unperturbed, stretched her arms upward and groaned as her muscles relaxed and then her arms fell to her lap.

Much more awake now, she stared at Roger.

"You know what, Roger? Clean it your fucking self."

"The Rebound"

We arrived at the cabin at around dusk, just as a slight, cool wind sent thousands of dead fall leaves eastward across the driveway from the mountains and into the valley below. I had driven the few hours to the rental while Cindy and Lisa chatted each other up the entire way. I doubted I'd said more than two words since we left the city.

Mainly, the drive was fraught with high drama. Lisa was still sniffling in the backseat when I pulled in the driveway of the two-story, pre-fab monster of a faux wood truss cabin, built by yuppie developers snow-birding in Florida, no doubt.

"...I just can't believe that son of a bitch. After all these years. What do I not have that she has?" she asked.

"She doesn't have anything you don't have, sweetie," Cindy reassured her. "He's reached that age where he's hit a mid-life crisis and that's that."

"But...John hasn't done that to *you*," she contended.

"In all fairness, I haven't hit the middle of my life *yet*," I responded and immediately regretted every syllable as Cindy gave me the stink-eye from the passenger seat.

"I mean, I'm just *clarifying*," I stammered as I looked outside and tried to make like I was focused on the orange and red of the fall's heyday brilliance.

"Well, you'd best clarify a little differently," Cindy said but then turned back to Lisa. "Look, let's just have a good time. That's what this trip is all about. We're getting away from the kids and you get to forget about him for a bit. It's 'us' time and 'you' time and that's okay."

Lisa's lowered lip quaked. "And thank you...thank you both so much for showing me this courtesy. I know it was your weekend."

I groaned on the inside—having been at least somewhat cock-blocked—but my better nature caused me to say, "You're a friend. We've known you for twenty years. This isn't some kind of special favor. We're just friends helping each other out. Now, let's go check out the cabin."

We hopped out. There were no neighbors around and you could see the natural haze of the Great Smoky Mountains in all directions through the trees.

"I'll be fine," Lisa declared. "I'm strong. I can get through this."

"Yes, you can, sweetie," Cindy said as she wrapped her arm around her. "Let's go have a drink right now! No more crocodile tears!"

They led the way arm-in-arm as I was relegated to carrying in the luggage. They both unnecessarily brought along a good four bags.

Regardless of the struggle, I could not help but focus on their asses as they walked onto the breezeway of the cabin and to the front door. Both wore tight Yoga pants and black leather jackets. Both were busty brunettes with long, flowing dark hair. Lisa was a few years older than Cindy, but the difference was unnoticeable. They were classically beautiful with relentless, hourglass figures.

We entered the cabin and found our rooms upstairs before reconvening in the game room where there was a pool table and a bar. I stood behind the bar in an quasi-official capacity.

"Whaddya have, ladies?" I asked professionally.

They seated themselves at the bar stools and played along. "I'll have my usual, bartender," Cindy said. "Not sure about my friend."

"Give me something strong. As strong as you can make it," Lisa requested.

I decided to forego the jigger and eyeballed the proper quantities of the drinks, although my procedure varied between the two. With Cindy, I made her amaretto sour conscientiously, making sure that I did not overdo the booze. With Lisa, I attempted an Old Fashioned but suddenly forgot all the ingredients, so her rocks glass was filled mainly with straight bourbon.

I turned on some hard rock and watched them drink. Lisa did not seem to notice the potency of her drink and chugged it down, every few minutes chiming in something like "that motherfucker" and "his dick was so small, what do I care anyway?"

I racked 'em.

"Anybody care for a game?"

Cindy and Lisa looked back.

"What are we playing?" Lisa asked.

"I don't care. Eight Ball?"

"Better fix those balls right then," Lisa said as she hopped down from her stool and rearranged them accordingly.

Cindy watched Lisa beat me handily in the first match. She would shoot, drink, shoot, drink, shoot, drink. Her first drink led into two more.

By the third game, she was missing shots she'd previously made but seemed to care a lot less.

"Ohh, you fuckers, I don't know what I'm doing wrong here," she complained to the balls as she scratched aiming the 5-ball into the side pocket, losing her balance and missing the ball entirely.

Cindy laughed with each subsequently missed shot. She had initially sipped her amaretto sour but by the time Lisa had scratched in the fourth game, I had noticed her take two shots of tequila.

"Ughhhh, I'm over it. My pool skills suck just like my love life," Lisa exclaimed as she fell back into a leather love seat. "Roll us a big fatty, John," she said.

"Sure thing."

The fireplace roared in the rec room as I whipped out a quarter bag of dank and broke up the buds, extracting the tiny stems like a surgeon. There were no seeds. I pulled out a pack of

ZigZags and rolled a veritable "hog leg" so large pot kept spilling out of both ends.

"Do the honors," I told Lisa, and she obliged, lighting the doobie.

"I hope all my anxiety goes up in smoke. I don't like rejection. The silence is the worst. I'd rather argue all day with a son of a bitch than sitting in silence alone with my thoughts. I have to stay distracted. I'm not ready to confront it all just yet," she said as she inhaled deeply and then began hacking uncontrollably for about five minutes.

"Good shit, good shit," she said as she made her hand into a fist and thumped on her chest.

The doobie made its way around the rotation three times until she became completely stoned and three-quarters drunk. Cindy noticed me take her tiny puffs like a 12-year-old with his old man's cigarettes, blushed, and then gave me a wink and smile as she deliberately looked down at the bulge in my pajama bottoms.

"Good god, why are we inside?" Lisa asked, looking out on the deck overlooking the mountains. "There's a perfectly good hot tub out there and there's nobody in it. That's a problem."

She stood, wavering, and then made her way out the glass doors.

"Hey, Lisa, don't you want to change into your suit?" Cindy asked.

"Oh hell no, this looks too good out here. I'm sorry, Cin, but your man is about to see me naked."

Cindy looked at me and emitted a faint, baffled chuckle. Lisa began pulling away at her t-shirt and bra.

"Come on, you two get out here!"

Lisa was short, standing about five feet and an inch or two. But she had an impressive bust that her clothes had unfortunately obscured all these years. She jerked her comfy pants down with her red thong panties, revealing a healthy but trimmed bush.

Cindy and I made our way outside.

"Lose those clothes," she said to us both.

I looked at Cindy and awaited some instructions. She

leaned in and whispered in my ear.

"She's beyond sad. Let's do this and make her forget about him for a while. It's fine."

My adrenaline surged as Cindy unbuttoned her top and lost her clothes. Her skin was olive-colored, and her areolas were large and round. Her nipples pointed straight outward and could have cut glass by the looks of them. It was only around forty degrees.

Lisa relaxed in the hot tub while we were unclothing. I got all the way to my boxers before the bashfulness set in and I submerged myself with my underwear still on, following Cindy into the hot tub where Lisa was waiting.

"Oh, don't be a pussy," she said as I stepped down into the hot tub. It felt amazing and my skin crawled as I sat opposite Lisa and Cindy and we sat looking out into the dark, cold night.

Cindy and Lisa kept giggling, clearly stoned. I had a head-change myself but was nowhere near their level.

At one point, Lisa leaned into Cindy and whispered something, both turning to me and giggling.

"What's so funny?"

"I was just sitting here telling your wife you've probably jerked off thinking about this exact situation."

"Well, there's the old Lisa. Dirty and pervy. That's what I'm used to," I said.

"It's a little weird that I used to be your manager and tell you to flip burgers all day and here we all are now, after all this time," Lisa said.

"All this time..." I spoke.

"Something I've been wondering," Cindy said. "Did you two ever fuck when you worked together?"

Lisa spit her drink out. "No, no, no. He was a senior in high school when I was his manager, plus you were dating. I would never have done that."

"Me, either," I lied.

Cindy laughed. "I love you both. I was just wondering. I'm not going to lie. I've wondered about it before and gotten insanely jealous and now the thought kind of turns me on. It must be me getting older and less inhibited."

"I mean, we *are* great friends," Lisa said. "I think our relationship would not get damaged if we ever wanted to try something different like that."

Cindy stared at Lisa and Lisa stared back. I felt my heart in my throat and my cock had gotten hard from the sheer tension of the situation.

Cindy toyed with Lisa's hair and then they locked their lips. Cindy put her arm around Lisa and both made out, their tongues in each other's mouth. They embraced closer.

"Come over," Cindy said to me, and I obliged. I scooted over and sat by Cindy. "No, by Lisa."

Surprised, I moved over beside Lisa, watching their enormous breasts pressed up against each other.

"Stroke his cock, baby," she said to Lisa. Lisa turned her head to me.

"Let me see it, John."

I took off the boxers and threw them out into the woods, both having a laugh. Cindy reached down in the warm water and gripped my cock forcefully. "Oh, fuck," I gasped.

Cindy had leaned Lisa's head down into her bosom, where Lisa licked all over Cindy's nipples while Lisa stroked my cock slowly. Cindy and I locked eyes, enjoying each other through Lisa, both of us pleased by the other being pleased.

"Oh yeah, you do that so good. I always knew you could lick me like that," Cindy said to Lisa.

"Let's go inside," Lisa said and broke away the grasp on my cock suddenly.

Lisa and Cindy did not even grab a towel as they held hands and ran into the cabin, dripping a trail of water behind them. I followed behind, my hard-on making the walk extra difficult, waddling like a penguin.

They piled into the first bedroom they could find, and Cindy fell on top of Lisa. This time, it was Cindy's mouth on Lisa's nipples, which were only slightly smaller than Cindy's. I laid down beside them and watched as I stroked on my cock, watching these two beautiful, voluptuous women enjoy each other.

Cindy slowly began kissing down her belly and eased down to her pelvic area. She kissed all around her pussy without touching any part of it, kissing on her hips, her inner thighs. Lisa kept widening her legs, throbbing for Cindy until she eventually grabbed the back of Cindy's head and plunged Cindy's head into her pussy.

Cindy looked up and watched me jerk my cock and gave a little head nod in Lisa's direction. I turned and found Lisa already staring at me as she rubbed all over her big tits. She offered up her right tit to me and I began licking away. Cindy was grasping Lisa's ass in both hands as she licked all over Lisa's clit but released it with her left hand as she began stroking me. Some pre-cum had drizzled out and Cindy put it on Lisa's clit so she could lick it off.

Lisa and I locked tongues as I massaged her breasts, squeezing lightly on her nipples. She moaned as I kissed her and would grind her pussy into Cindy's face as Cindy began stroking me faster.

Cindy stopped abruptly. "I want you to fuck my husband."

Lisa hesitated for just one sec and then I nodded. She mounted me, rubbing her clit against my cock without putting it inside her. Cindy approached Lisa from the back and began eating her ass as she cupped and stroked my balls.

Cindy grabbed my cock from underneath and inserted it inside Lisa, both of us moaning as it penetrated her deeply and forcefully. Cindy made her way to a chair and sat back, watching Lisa's big tits bounce as she began fingering her pussy. I felt Lisa's ass bounce on my balls as she came down each time.

Cindy and I stared at each other, and I noticed how wet my wife was watching me fuck our friend. Lisa fell forward and I put both of her nipples in my mouth, licking both simultaneously as I squeezed on her ass.

Cindy came back to bed and licked all over my balls, cleaning all of Lisa's pussy juice off me. She then sat on my face, and I began licking her pussy inside and out while she made out with Lisa. The room was nothing but moans and the sweet stench of sex, ethyl alcohol, and weed.

Lisa and Cindy dismounted, and Lisa went down on Cindy. I put my cock in Cindy's mouth as she laid on her back blowing me while getting her pussy eaten. She hummed as she sucked me, the vibrations making me tingle.

Her body tensed and she orgasmed with my cock in her mouth, pulling away to scream as she pushed Cindy away from her, contorting into an asymmetrical ball on the bad, cumming so much she did not know what to do with herself.

"Fuck her...fuck her...f-f-f-fuck her. I need a minute."

Lisa was still in a doggy position from eating Cindy, so I approached her from behind and inserted myself, fucking her doggy style rapidly, her pussy juice flying everywhere. Cindy listened to her friend squall and came again, not even watching us, but just listening.

I pushed Lisa down on her belly into a prone position and straddled her thigh while I fucked her from behind. I pounded on her pussy, for years speculating how good it would feel and the reality matching up to expectations, for once. Those years had accumulated, and all the lust and wonder overwhelmed me as I squeezed both of her ass cheeks and fucked her, penetrating all the way into her.

"Choke me. Choke me," she commanded and before I could attempt to do so, Cindy slid over and pressed herself against Lisa, reaching around her throat with one hand and fingering her ass with the other. Lisa widened her position to open her pussy more to me and her ass to Cindy. Lisa's moans were gurgled as Cindy choked her.

Cindy broke away and crawled to me.

"Let me taste your cock."

I pulled out of Lisa and Cindy immediately began licking all up and down my cock. Lisa turned like a swivel and began kissing Cindy's neck as Cindy blew me. Lisa began toying with my balls with her tongue as my wife deepthroated me.

"I've always wanted you two. Oh my god, this is so hot," said Lisa as they began making out with the head of my cock between them. They fingered each other until Lisa came, arching her back, showing her big tits off to us. She fell on the bed, her orgasm lingering.

"How do you want to cum, baby?" Cindy asked me.

So many possibilities made my head swim, and despite years thinking of this very circumstance, I felt indecisive.

"I know," Cindy said. "I want you to cum in her."

Lisa and I looked at each other and she bit on her lower lip as she spread her legs open for me. Her bush and pussy looked beautiful in the lamp light as I went down on her while her orgasm persisted. She wailed as I licked on her clit tenderly and then put myself into missionary, burying my cock in her.

Cindy laid back and fingered herself.

"Cum in me. Let me have that cum, baby," Lisa begged. "I want it. I want it so bad. Fill me up."

"Do it. Fucking cum in her pussy. Breed her, baby," Cindy said.

Watching them both stroke their tits, I thrust my cock in as deeply as I could go and felt my orgasm peak as I flooded her pussy with my cum. Cindy welcomed it and pulled me in tighter, embracing the cum, her pussy contracting.

I pulled out, saving one last string of cum to shoot across Lisa's body, and it shot from her bushy pussy to her throat and chin. She giggled, surprised. Her body, writhing.

Cindy was right there and licked the cum right off Lisa's face, tits, stomach, and pussy.. She didn't swallow but hovered over Lisa. Lisa opened her mouth as Cindy opened hers' and let the cum fall down into her mouth. Lisa gulped the cum down and embraced Cindy and both held out their arms so I would join them as the three of us embraced, eventually falling sound asleep, Cindy and I snuggled up to Lisa on both sides.

"No Pretending Here"

We pulled into the Smith's driveway right at dusk, and I could see that Mark already had a roaring fire going in his backyard behind his log-cabin style house. Courtney was sitting in a wooden lounge chair beneath the trees that were shedding its final autumn leaves. She turned her head and smiled as she saw us pull up. Mark stood to the side in a light jacket, his black and grey hair pulled back into a bun, drinking a beer from a dark bottle. He nodded and smiled as we pulled in, as well.

"Do we need a cue to get out of here? Maybe say you have a headache or something?" I asked Cindy as I put the car in "park."

"We'll see," she said. "They've tried to get us out here forever. Let's at least pretend to have a good time."

"I will give it a good faith effort."

"I should hope so. I don't want any awkwardness between us at school functions."

"Nor I."

"All the same," Cindy added, "I'll fake a phone call from the babysitter if it gets unbearable."

"Agreed."

Mark and Courtney were both former military, a few years younger than us. Mark stood well over six feet and Courtney was tall and lean. Neither seemed to have any fat on their bodies and were well-built. Courtney had darker blonde hair and freckles.

"Come on over," Mark said immediately after we got out of the car and began to approach them. "It's just about time you two stopped making excuses and agreed to have dinner."

"Excuses?" I asked. "If that's what you can call kids, chores, and a career. We even have to make an effort to schedule date nights these days."

"Oh, I know. We're in the same boat. Your mom got the kids?" he asked Cindy.

"She does. Neither are feeling well, though, so we'll see how the night goes," Cindy replied. I gave her a look only she and I could have discerned, as I was proud of her for laying the foundation for an escape following dinner.

A brilliant scent hit my nostrils. "Whatcha cookin', Mark?"

"I'm smoking brisket with some corn-on-the-cob and beans from our garden."

"Damn, did you brew that beer you're drinking, too?"

"Actually, I did. One of the hobbies we have around the farm."

"Are you *sure* you're in the same boat as we are? I barely have time to load the dishwasher."

"Oh, you've just got to make time for the things you enjoy, John," Courtney poked with a wink.

We sat around the fire in silence for a bit and watched Mark stoke the fire. Cindy sat by Courtney, and I looked at them from across the fire. Cindy was curvy with dark black hair tempered with blond highlights. I could not help by "size her up" in relation to Courtney and vice versa. There was no one I was more attracted to than Cindy, who I had been with since I was sixteen, and she eighteen. But Courtney was undoubtedly attractive, as well. Cindy was shorter, more voluptuous, with big, mysterious eyes. She was busty and could not hide that fact beneath her fall sweater.

By contrast, Courtney had smaller breasts and longer legs. She and Mark both had several tattoos, a few indicating their time in the Marines.

"Can I offer you guys a drink?" Mark asked.

"I'm thinking just a coffee," Cindy said. "If you have any."

"You don't want anything stronger?" Courtney asked. I noticed her take a long drink from a Yeti. "I've had a few Bloody Mary's today, if you want."

"Well..." Cindy looked in my direction. "You driving us home tonight if I indulge?"

"Yes, ma'am," I responded.

"I'd like a screwdriver if you have any OJ."

"Can do!" said Courtney. "How about you, John?"

"I'll take some of that coffee and maybe a doobie from all that pot you guys grow in that greenhouse back there."

Both laughed as if I had said the most hysterical thing ever, as was their way. I'd never really seen them in a bad mood at parent events.

"How come you always try and get me into trouble?" Mark asked jokingly.

"Youuuuu," Courtney said, "can get into trouble all by yourself." She walked over and kissed Mark. She was tall, but he had to bend down to kiss her. She wrapped her arms around him, and the kiss lingered. I felt uneasy and looked at Cindy. She watched them with a tiny smile and seemed undisturbed.

"Sorry about that," Courtney said. "There honestly aren't too many nights we get away from the kids, either. Plus, I've had a couple of these to drink in the last little bit."

I waved the apology away. "No problem at all. Honestly, though, I'm jealous of how fit and straight-laced you two seem so I like to bring you down to my level."

"Oh, we are totally out of shape compared to when we were in the Corps," Mark said.

"What, like you run a seven-minute mile now instead of a six-minute mile?"

We ate dinner on their back porch, which was delicious. Cindy, surprisingly, went through four screwdrivers with relative ease, which was unusual. Mark kept drinking his homebrew while Courtney kept putting down those wretched Bloody Mary's.

The conversation progressed from school and the kids to parenting and then to a collective bitch fest about inching toward middle adulthood, in the place of our parents. I abstained from any drinks, at one point excusing myself to the bathroom and took a few puffs from a marijuana vape that took the edge off.

When I returned, the conversation had seemed to die down, and Cindy excused herself to the bathroom. I fully anticipated this would be when she would return with an excuse to leave. I was surprised when she did not when she returned, helping Courtney clear the table while Mark and I lit some cigars, our joint offer at helping declined.

He again stoked the fire, and we sat staring at the clear night sky. We didn't talk much, just comfortably enjoying the silence.

Eventually, he said, "I feel like they've been inside for a while. You think they're ever coming back?"

"I dunno. I was getting curious about that myself."

"Let go see what they're getting into."

We found them in the basement, which doubled for an informal living room and workspace for Courtney's photography. Cindy and Courtney were walking around looking at Courtney's work that graced her walls.

"These are *amazing*," Cindy said.

"Thank you. I've really been working at it, trying to make it a full-time job."

I then noticed we were looking at boudoir pictures, and several different women and couples scantily clad were portrayed therein.

"I've always wanted to try this. I just get so insecure getting older and all," Cindy lamented.

"There's no reason for that," Courtney assured her. "You have a beautiful body."

Mark and I traded sly glances at each other, no amount of hospitality and civility having any chance compared to testosterone.

"You should let me some take snaps," Courtney said.

"What—here? Right now?"

"Yes. I have different outfits in that walk-in over there. I never know exactly what my clients might like."

"Is that okay, John?"

"It's entirely up to you. I don't have any other plans."

"Well, come in here and pick something out with me."

"Okay."

The closet was a sample across the spectrum of leather and lace, classy and risqué. I entered behind Cindy and began considering the options when she abruptly put her hand on my cock, rubbing against it on the outside of my jeans. She thrust her tongue in my mouth so forcefully I almost fell back into a rack of sexy onesies.

"Oh my god, I'm so fucking horny," Cindy said, her breasts pressed against me, with her grinding against my cock. "I guess I drank too much."

"It's fine. It's awesome. I spun her around and pressed myself against her ass, wrapping my hand around her neck and tilting her head back so I could kiss her from behind.

"Pick me out something."

"Yes, ma'am."

My hands shook at the thought of fucking her in the room next to another couple. I could barely search through the racks of teddies, corsets, and hosiery.

I eventually—very selectively chosen, given the level of my adrenaline—picked out a garment. I took it off the rack and showed it to her.

"Oh my, you want me to wear that?"

"I do. I'm dying for that."

"I dunno…"

"Do it."

"Go in there while I put it on."

When I emerged from the closet, Courtney had changed into gym shorts and a sleeveless top, revealing her muscular, tattooed arms. Mark sat on a couch with his boots and jacket off, in a white t-shirt. Her arms were equally muscular and tatted.

Courtney had turned on some track lights in a small corner of the basement. The track lighting illuminated a golden chaise lounge chair and a black backdrop.

"Grab a seat. Get comfortable," Courtney said. I sat next to Mark.

Cindy emerged in a black, see-through flyaway gown and a G-string. She had on long stiletto heels and her hair was up in a bun. Mark, Courtney, and I all three gazed upon her without blinking. Her nipples stood erect, and I immediately began to get hard staring at her.

"Oh my god," Courtney said. "You're hot."

"Ummm, is this a 'girl's only" kind of affair?" Mark asked, looking at me.

"I don't mind if she doesn't," I answered.

Cindy, blushing, looked at Courtney the same way Mark had looked at me and Courtney laughed. "I definitely don't mind. We're not the jealous type."

"Where do you want me?" asked Cindy.

"Over on the chaise."

"What should I do?"

"Whatever feels natural. Be fun and spontaneous."

"I may need another drink."

"I think we all might need a drink," Mark said.

"Yeah, I think I'm ready," I concurred.

Courtney brought over shots, and I smelled the Tequila before it even got close. We all took the shots, and then Cindy laid down on the chaise, posing with one arm daintily laid across her head while she stared into the camera. She gazed over at me and Mark and smiled and eventually the blush went away.

Courtney's professional-grade camera kept flashing as she danced around the room, snapping Cindy in different angles. Every few minutes, she would say, "Switch!" and Cindy would very fluidly adapt a new position. She laid down on her belly and raised her hips up and back a few times. She stood and bent over the back of the chaise.

I had never seen her like this.

We downed more shots.

Eventually, she returned to her original position, a little tipsier than when she began. As she flopped back into the chaise, her G-string must have been just a little too big on her, and when she stretched out, it dropped to one side, revealing her landing strip and her pussy.

"Oh god, sorry," she said, laughingly, and covered herself with a half-effort. We all followed suit and laughed, with no embarrassment.

Eventually, the flashes of lights diminished. Courtney put her camera down.

"I think...I think we just need an adjustment with your hair, okay? Do you mind if I come over there and fix you up?"

"Not at all," Cindy replied. She turned on her side and rested her head against her palm, with her legs semi-spread. The G-string had fallen to the side again and she made no effort to cover herself this time.

Courtney knelt beside her and brushed her hair back on one side with her hand and then undid the clip that held her hair up. Her dark hair fell and as it did, Cindy and Courtney both seemed to simultaneously—and aggressively—lock their lips together. They French kissed as if Mark and I were not even in the room, and tiny moans of passion echoed through the basement.

Cindy grabbed Courtney's hand and put it on her hip. Courtney squeezed and rubbed her ass while they alternated kissing each other's lips and necks. I was so hard it was painfully rubbing against my jeans. When I turned to Mark to check his reaction, I noticed his cock was already out and he was stroking it softly.

"Are you cool with all this?" he whispered.

I nodded and unzipped my pants and took my cock out, as well. When I looked up again, the women were now watching us, and Courtney had slid her fingers down to my wife's clit and was stroking it both delicately and assertively. Cindy's hips seemed to pulsate with each little flicker.

"Let me see those tits," she said to Courtney. Courtney pulled her shirt off, showing breasts that were larger than what they appeared from her clothed. She had a farmer's tan from all her outside work. She pulled down her shorts and had no panties. She saw Mark and I staring and wiggled her ass at us.

"Just enjoy the view, boys," she said. She then grabbed Cindy's leg and flung it to one side, revealing her entire pussy to us. Cindy kicked her heels off. Courtney crept down and put her face in Cindy's pussy. Cindy moaned loudly the second Courtney's tongue contacted her clit. I could see how wet she was from twelve feet away. Cindy toyed with her nipples and rubbed her tits while Courtney flicked her tongue up-and-down and sideways on her clit. She grabbed her ass with both her hands and did not slow for a second.

She opened her eyes and watched Mark and I stroke our cocks. There was so much pre-cum all over both of us we might as well had rubbed lube all over ourselves.

Abruptly, Cindy stopped and stood up.

"Let's go. Right now," she said to all of us. She helped Cindy up and Cindy followed behind her holding her hand, to the guest bedroom in the basement. I followed Cindy and she looked back at me. I nodded approvingly of what was to happen.

When we entered the bedroom, Courtney turned Cindy around and immediately began making out with her while they were standing. She slipped Cindy out of the rest of her lingerie and then playfully pushed Cindy back on the bed.

"We've never done this before," Cindy said to Courtney and Mark.

I patted my belly. "I guess I'm a little insecure, too."

"You're beautiful. Both of you. Come on."

Courtney turned down the lighting and Cindy rolled to the middle of the bed. I pulled down my pants and my boxers and climbed in the bed beside her. I noticed Courtney blowing Mark as he took off his shirt. He grabbed the back of her hair and guided her speed.

I kissed Cindy but I knew by her movements and the way her body writhed that she was ready for more, already on the verge of cumming. My cock was aching with want and I got on top of her in missionary position. I toyed with her clit with the head of my cock and each time she pulled me to try and make me penetrate her, I resisted. I felt her squirt all over me, and I had never experienced this from her.

Mark and Courtney approached Cindy from both sides of the side and began licking her nipples.

"Oh, fuuuccckkk. Oh my god, this feels so fuckin' good," Cindy bellowed, grabbing onto the back of Mark's man-bun and Courtney's ponytail. She quivered and as I barely slid inside her, she cried out with an orgasm, tears falling from its intensity as she screamed. I kept pounding on her as she came but the convergence of her nipples being licked and being fucked at the same time was too much and she pushed Mark and Cindy away. I stayed deep inside her and didn't back off.

Meanwhile, Mark laid down by Cindy and began caressing her nipples while Courtney began riding him, putting her right beside me. She watched me watch her fucking her husband and pulled my head down into her perky tits, where I began licking all over her nipples. Cindy guided Mark's hand down to her clit and he fingered her there while I pounded on her pussy, her orgasm continuing, where we remained for some time.

"Let's try something," Courtney said as she hopped off Mark. "I want you to lick my pussy, Cindy."

"Oh yes, fuck yes," Cindy said as Courtney positioned her perpendicular across the bed. Courtney straddled Cindy's face and it was the first time I'd ever seen her go down on a woman. I had to pause to catch myself from cumming—enjoying this way too much—before I again put my cock inside Cindy.

Mark simultaneously positioned herself behind Courtney and put his cock in Courtney with Courtney on top of Cindy in the "69" position. I looked down and Cindy licked all over Courtney's clit. Cindy's moans were muffled by Courtney grinding her hips into Cindy's face mercilessly. I felt Courtney reach down and play with my balls while I rapidly fucked Cindy.

Mark did the same, and I watched as he pulled out his large cock out—glistening wet from Courtney's pussy—and Cindy open her mouth for him. She licked all of Courtney's pussy juice of his cock and he thrust up and down so she could blow him from underneath Courtney. Courtney pulled my cock out of Cindy and began doing the same, "Mmmm, mmmm, mmmm, mmmm," were the noises coming from both of them. We alternated fucking them and pulling out our cocks to be sucked. I watched Mark getting blown by his wife and he watched me getting blown by his and we could see in each other's eyes how much we both enjoyed it.

"I want to ride you, John," Cindy said. Courtney climbed off. I laid down across the bed and Cindy got on top of me. She was drenched and I was soaked before she slid herself down on me. Courtney then straddled my face, and I began licking her pussy and she rode my face to the same rhythm as Cindy riding my cock.

Cindy and Courtney licked all over each other's nipples, with Courtney enjoying Cindy's large tits and Cindy enjoying Courtney's perky ones. They rubbed all over each other's asses— Cindy's curvy and beautiful, and Courtney's tight and beautiful.

I felt Mark beside me stroking his cock. He stood up and approached Cindy from behind. He stroked his cock right behind Cindy and I could barely see from his wife's pussy in my mouth, but I noticed that he was stroking his cock in one hand, and he had his hand around one of Cindy's tits with the other. He was jacking off with the head of his dick in-between Cindy's ass cheeks, but not penetrating.

I waved him on, and he slid his head in Cindy's ass.

"Oh, god, fuck me, fuck me, but go slow for a second. Oh fuck," Cindy cried out. Courtney hopped off my face and laid beside me, fingering her pussy while watching us double penetrate Cindy. Cindy leaned back against Mark as she rode me and wrapped her arm around his neck and pulled him in to kiss all over her neck. I felt his balls rub against mine as Cindy's rhythms in riding me matched his as he fucked her ass, each time getting deeper and deeper. Cindy rode and rode and collapsed against me, nearly at an orgasm again. I took one nipple in my mouth and Mark kept fucking her as she came again, biting down on my neck as she orgasmed.

She fell back at the foot of the bed, making Mark stumble

KAY LACEY

backward. She was panting and cumming, almost delirious with pleasure.

I didn't relent. I went over to Cindy and threw her over on her belly and pulled her ass up and began fucking her doggystyle. Mark did the same to Courtney. Courtney and Cindy made out as we fucked both. Courtney began shaking and screaming from Mark's big cock going deep in her pussy as he fingered her ass. When she came, her tongue was locked with Cindy's, and she made loud convulsing noises with each wave of her orgasm.

Courtney curled on the bed for a moment, and then went to a comfy chair in the corner. She brought out a realistic dildo and sat down.

"I want to watch. I know this is your first time, Cindy. I want you to enjoy yourself."

Mark laid on the bed, and put his cock between Cindy's big tits as I kept fucking her from behind. She squeezed his dick in between her tits and bounced playfully up and down on his cock, letting him titty-fuck her. She would stop at intervals and take his balls in one hand and suck on him as I pulled on her hair and spanked her ass. Courtney sat in the corner on the chair, masturbating with the dildo, enjoying long and deep penetrations.

Cindy was clearly enjoying the freedom of this position and playfully wiggled her ass on my cock and relentlessly let Mark titty-fuck her. I saw him try and slow her down, but she kept doing it even faster, and faster. He tried to stop her, but she wouldn't stop, grabbing the bottom of his cock with one hand to stroke and titty-fuck him at the same time. She giggled at she very obviously "tortured" Mark.

Mark couldn't handle it. With a grunt, he came suddenly, almost violently. His cum shot out across Cindy's face as she kept her speed up-and-down on his cock. His cum made a diagonal pattern across her face and all over her lips. It trickled down to her tits and Mark managed to wrest himself away from her, falling to the floor.

"That's so fucking hot, baby," I said to Cindy.

She turned. "I want your cum, too. Right now. Right fuckin' now."

"Cum all over your hot fuckin' wife, John," Courtney said from the corner.

I gave her one final spank on the ass and pulled out from her. She spun around. I saw all of the cum already on her and it drove me over the edge as I grabbed her by the back of the head and came across her lips. Courtney came over and put her face in Cindy's pussy one last time as I kept cumming. Courtney drove the fat dildo into Cindy's cunt while she spanked her and watched me cum.

Cindy fell back, covered in our cum, quivering. Mark was in the floor still quivering while Courtney hovered over Cindy and licked all our cum from Cindy's tits and face and the two locked lips in the final embrace of the night.

"Friendly Neighborhood BBC"

After two days of meddlesome eyes watching him unpack, I was the lone person from the neighborhood to introduce myself to Kareem from the *cul-de-sac*. Despite the buzz around the WASP-y neighborhood of the new arrival, no one had enough courage or courtesy to approach him.

I walked over from directly across the street on a Saturday. Kareem was tossing boxes off the back of his truck into the driveway. He was a large man, built well, standing well over six feet. His triceps and biceps jutted out from his white Polo shirt. He was clean-cut and sported a moustache and glasses. Sweat beaded up on his forehead and down his cheeks.

"Man, you need some help? I live just across the street. I'm off today and could help out," I offered.

Kareem looked up mid-lift.

"Nah, I think I got it now. 'Preciate the offer, though. Which house is yours'?"

I pointed to the Colonial directly behind us. His house was roughly the same—covered with stucco and faux stone, but maybe a different floor plan, like the rest of the houses up and down the street. Like the old song, these were definitely "little boxes made of ticky tacky."

"What brings you to the neighborhood?" I asked.

He put the box down and stood up, dusting his hands off. "New job. Old one downsized and had to take what I could. I've known computers all my life but for whatever reason these companies think youngsters with B.S. degrees are worth more than forty-year-olds with twenty years of experience."

"I hear ya. That's a shame."

"What do you do for a living?"

"I'm a lawyer. My wife stays at home and holds down the fort while I'm off at work, keeping the lights on. I feel ya about being forty. I feel completely capable, but people prefer the young bucks these days. Anybody came over here and introduced themselves?"

He grinned, knowingly. "Nah, not a one. A lot of rubberneckers but nobody has come around. I guess ya'll aren't used to a brotha on the block."

"Well, give them time. They're good folks. It just takes them a minute to warm up. Pretty soon your wife will be knee-deep in the neighborhood gossip, and you'll miss being left alone."

He hopped off the truck and held out his hand.

"I'm Kareem. No wife. Divorced. I guess you could say I'm married to be work."

"Same here. I try to have boundaries but it's difficult. Maybe if you have time in the afternoon, I'm having a small barbeque by the pool. Nothing formal. We're just sitting around and making the most of the summer before it's over. It's just a few friends. It would be a good segue into meeting a few people."

He considered it for a moment. "You gonna have beer over there?"

"I wouldn't dream of not having any beer at a summer barbeque. What kind do you drink?"

"Oh, I haven't ever met a beer I wouldn't drink but I prefer PBR."

I chuckled. "I have a fridge full of PBR in my garage. It's not what the yokels drink—they like Stella. But I'll bring out a dozen or so for us and put them in the cooler for ya."

"Nice. I appreciate that, as well. I'll be over in a few hours once I get some chores done and try to get settled. Not much time.

Starting work Monday. But I'll say hello. Is this neighborhood... accepting?"

"Oh, you'd be surprised. I'm John, by the way."

"Nice to meet you, John."

"See you soon."

I walked back home and found my wife in the backyard cleaning the grill. She'd already cleaned the pool and apparently had taken a dip. She wore a bikini, but her bottom was covered up by white shorts. Her breasts looked ample, and the sun reflected off her chest. Her dark hair was fixed up into two pigtails. Each swipe of her sponge on the grill caused her ass (which was ample, as well) to jiggle.

I stood at the back sliding door and just admired her figure for a few minutes until she looked up and saw me staring.

"Well, how'd that go?"

"Good. He's a nice guy. Kareem."

"Is he coming over?"

I grabbed a Stella out of the cooler and popped it open. "I think so. He's a little worried about prejudice it seems like."

Cindy stood with her hand on her hip. "Did you tell him we don't tolerate that kind of behavior?"

"More or less. Close enough. I made him feel welcome."

"Good. Hopefully these snooty little bitches around the neighborhood do the same. You gonna help me or sit around and drink?"

"You know what I love about you? Your honesty and directness." I came over and kissed her. She pressed herself against me. Despite the privacy fences, I could feel those meddlesome eyes staring down on us from the neighboring houses.

"Get to work, stud."

I did. I cleaned the house, vacuumed, swept, mopped,

strategically taking chugs of beer when I could.

I had showered and was reading the paper when the first doorbell rang. It was the Schwartz's. We had told everybody four and they arrived at 3:45, as was their way.

After pleasantries, we escorted them to the back and hung out around the pool, Ted Schwartz telling us about the exciting world of securities and Beth Schwartz swapping stories with Cindy about school rumors, as Cindy formerly taught with Beth at the local high school.

More arrived—the Donaldsons, the Smiths, and the Walkers. They arrived and each came with either a tray of food or a bottle of wine. These weren't really my people, but it was good to maintain study neighborhood relations. These were political relationships, made to ensure a well-oiled neighborhood. "No man is an island," that kind of thing.

Eventually, Kareem arrived. He didn't bring a bottle with him or a tray of food. He brought a container full of summer sausages and cheeses.

"Hot damn," I exclaimed upon greeting him. "Let's break these out in my garage. There's plenty of food for the crowd. They'll be okay without this."

We cut up the sausages and blocks of cheese and took them out to the garage, half of which I'd converted to my "man cave" with a fridge, coffee table, gigantic TV, and two recliners. On occasion, I'd smoke grass out there and pretend it was my father's garage back in the day and that I was sixteen again.

"Wanna watch the ballgame?"

"Oh, most definitely," he replied.

We both stretched out on the two recliners and drank PBR and ate the sausages, crackers, and cheeses on the coffee table between us. We watched the game, wise-cracking and telling fishing stories. Eventually, Cindy found her way to the man cave.

"Well, hello Kareem, I'm Cindy. It's great to meet you."

Kareem stood and shook her hand. By this point, she'd changed into a sundress and tan hat. She had on dark shades and her hair was still in pigtails, hanging down on either shoulder and onto her breasts.

"Nice to meet you, Cindy. Thank you for the invite to the party."

"Well, you're not even at the party! Don't worry, Kareem. I'm mad at my husband and not you. You two need to go socialize."

We let out a collective groan and made our way out back. We followed Cindy, whose ass swung horizontally and I wondered how it managed to miss hitting both walls as she walked. I watched Kareem stare.

All the couples were either lounging by the pool or under the palapa where we had a mini-bar. There were platefuls of brisket, baked beans, potato salad, burgers, dogs, and chips. The neighbors drank Stella and Appletinis and spoke loudly about local happenings and politics. When Kareem approached, they all were polite and bade him to sit with them. In the corner of my eye, I could see Cindy and Beth watch Kareem. Beth whispered in Cindy's ear and I noticed Cindy giggle a little and then nod her head in approval. I stood watching the conversations with a beer in my hand until I felt Cindy's hand on my back, massaging me.

I half-turned and saw her smile, looking at me but also at Kareem. She whispered in my ear: "Did you mean what we talked about the other night?"

"I did," I replied. "Are you interested?"

"I am. Very much so. I wasn't for sure if it was just dirty talk."

"It wasn't."

"Then, maybe we'll see how the day goes. Maybe him moving in next door is fortuitous for us."

"Chill out with the vocab lesson, teach. I'm drinkin', not studying for the GRE."

The afternoon slowly evaporated into evening, but the early September sun kept beating down on everybody. At one point, all the couples were in the pool together and Kareem hopped in, too.

He and I raced to the deep end of the pool and both relaxed once we got there.

"You're a lucky man, John. Your wife is gorgeous," he said, watching her from across the pool. She sat on the steps and spoke with the Walkers and Beth, every now and again glancing back in our direction.

"You know, 'you're a lucky man' is code for 'I'd fuck your wife,' Kareem," I joked.

Kareem took a moment and observed my face until he was sure I was joking and then laughed heartily.

"Well, it is what it is, I suppose," he said.

Eventually, as darkness slowly reared its head, couples started leaving, but not Kareem. He and I were engaged in a half-drunken discussion of whether Larry Bird or Magic was the better player.

"Look at the rings. Just look at the rings. That's all you got to look at. It doesn't matter how good Bird is, Magic has the most rings and that's that," he said.

"Larry can't carry a whole friggin' team. Magic had guys around him. Magic stood on their shoulders. Larry did it virtually all on his own."

"Now now, boys," Cindy said as she approached us. All the neighbors had left "I'm sure there's better things to talk about then sports."

"Well, it's probably about time I head out anyway. I've had a great time but it's getting late."

"Oh no," I said. "You're not leaving until you see my setup I have downstairs."

Downstairs, we'd fashioned a spare bedroom into a movie theater. Surrounding the huge projection screen I had adorned the walls with photography of great sports figures, one of which was Magic Johnson, whose picture was the largest in the room.

"Just so you don't think I'm being narrow-minded. I don't have anything of Bird's in here, but I have that of Magic. He was a great player."

Cindy watched us look at the memorabilia from the den outside the theater room. She reclined back on the couch and took off her hat. She dimmed the lights low with the remote.

"Is that all you two can talk about is sports?" she asked.

Kareem exited the room and sat down on the couch with Cindy.

"What else should we talk about?" he asked.

Cindy looked at me and nodded.

"Maybe we could talk about how you want to fuck my wife, Kareem," I said. His head shot up and his eyes grew as round as half dollars.

"WHAT? I didn't say that. I didn't say that at all. Don't embarrass me."

"So...you wouldn't fuck me, Kareem? John and I are getting older. We're getting more comfortable with ourselves and what turns us on. I've been wanting a big, black cock in my life for as long as I can remember. If you're not game, that's fine. If you're into it, that's even better."

Kareem watched her as she spread her legs wide, revealing no panties underneath her sun dress. Her pussy spread open, revealing her wetness and her clit.

"So, I'll ask it again: Would you fuck me?" she inquired yet again.

Kareem looked away from her and to me. I could see it in his eyes he wanted my approval, but he said nothing.

"John doesn't mind," Cindy said as she scooted over to him, and straddled him on the couch.

"Just stop me if you don't want me," she said, and began dry humping him, slowly while kissing his neck. Kareem reached out and squeezed on her plump ass, an "ohhhh" emitting from Cindy.

She pulled her top off and undid her bikini top, letting him see her big breasts and round, perfect nipples. He put his mouth on her right nipple and began licking as she humped him. She leaned her head back and savored his every flicker. I had my cock out already and approached them. Cindy began blowing me as Kareem licked her.

She squirmed away and kneeled in the floor, unzipping his pants. His cock was huge—a good 10" easily. Cindy took the head in her hand right hand and licked the precum off his cock. I sat down beside Kareem and stroked while she sucked him.

She would alternate sucking and then licking all over his shaft and balls, his cock looking huge in her tiny mouth. I became so hard watching her it felt like my cock was going to explode. She sucked him fast and deep and tried to deep throat him but could not.

"Gluck-gluck-gluck-gluck," were the sounds she made as she tried to fit all of his massive cock in her mouth. She stared up at him with her dark eyes as he grabbed a pigtail in each hand and loosened up some, his nerves slowly disappearing.

She straddled him again, this time putting his cock in her. "Oh fuuucckkkk, you're so fuckin' big. Oh my god, you're so fucking big. You like this, honey? You like watching me fucking his big dick?"

"I fucking love it," I said as I jerked harder and faster and played with my balls. Cindy rode him slowly and deeply, but did not let all of his dick go into her. She did this a few times until

Kareem, overcome with her movemt, grabbed her shoulders and pulled her down on him, all of his big cock up in her pussy.

"OH, GOD!" she said as he began forcefully fucking her. He did not relent and pounded on her pussy from underneath. He squeezed her ass and fingered it. I came over and licked all over her ass and asshole as she fucked him. Her ass was drenched with her cum.

She orgasmed as she rode him and clutched at his back when she hit her peak, scratching him as she screamed. When he finished, she fell off of him into the floor, writhing.

Kareem mounted her and I watched as he slid his cock into her all the way. Cindy seemed almost semi-conscious, each insertion making her big tits jiggle.

"God, I need your cum. I want your cum."

"I'm not near finished with you, ma'am," Kareem said as he flipped her over with ease. She laid in the prone position as he fucked her, his muscles on his arms and torso looking massive and sweaty.

She grimaced with each movement, and I could tell she was getting sore. Kareem noticed too, and slowed down his penetrations.

"I love that big, black cock. I love it," she said with her eyes closed. He bent her up and put her face in the carpet, with her ass up and fucked her doggystyle. Cindy tried to raise herself up but kept falling down on her face as he hands would not support herself.

Kareem slowly fucked her and spanked her ass. Her cheeks became blood red.

"Oh god, yes. Nice and slow. Spank my ass. Squeeze it. Oh my...oh my...oh my GOD!" she exclaimed as she orgasmed surprisingly. Her body tightened and relaxed, tightened, and relaxed.

"Bust in me. Bust in me!" she commanded.

"Are you on anything?" Kareem asked.

"No, but I don't care! I don't care. Do it, do it!"

"Do it, Kareem," I told him."

With a loud, guttural bellow, Kareen inserted himself to the hilt, grabbing onto her hips and thrusting her back at the same time as he flooded her pussy.

Cindy wailed, "Ohhhhh, ohhhhh, ohhhh…" and drifted off into a higher state of consciousness.

Kareem sat back and rested with his hands propping him, grinning smugly.

"That's the way it's done, son," he declared proudly.

"Oh yeah? Watch this, Magic Johnson."

Cindy lay askew, her body still semi-contorted. I slid my hand down in between her legs and lathered my hands in his cum and her juices generously and then lubed my cock. Staring at Kareem, I slid my head into her ass, stirring Cindy, who began "whoo-whooing" like an owl.

Simultaneously, I began playing with her clit, slowly, methodically, while plunging into her ass. It was tight and squeezed and the world around me lost all importance as I focused on that tightness and enjoyed each centimeter of her body.

I picked up speed and her body gyrated with each thrust. I looked at Kareem and he had begun to get hard again watching us. Cindy opened her eyes and nodded for him to bring his cock to her mouth. She sucked on it, her top half twisted upward while her bottom half stayed prone. This position opened her up fully to me.

She reached deep down and came to life again while I fucked her. Kareem's eyes were rolling back, his manhood still super sensitive from having cum just a few minutes prior. She sucked up and down his shaft and cupped his balls. "Mmm mmm mmm," came from Cindy, and I knew what that felt like—to have her beautiful mouth all over your cock and then her vibrations from moaning adding a heightened pleasure.

I fucked her rapidly as she blew Kareem to the same beat. I knew she was on the verge of cumming as her body tensed up. I gave her one deep thrust into her ass, and she hiked her leg slightly, squirting a good four feet away from us. Cumming intensely, she could no longer manage to suck on Kareem. She gripped his cock, her hand only making it halfway around its circumference, and involuntarily tightened her grip as her orgasm hit her in wave after wave.

Kareem, unable to contain himself from that extra pressure, burst, a shot of cum making its way across Cindy lips, cheek, and down on her tit. Kareem folded like a blanket you'd toss in the floor, heaving.

As I watched him to make sure he was still breathing, I blew in Cindy's ass, deeply, jerking out only somewhat to make sure to bust in her pussy, reclaiming her for myself. Her orgasm lingered as Kareem's fizzled out. He stood up quickly and grasped his clothes, making his way for the steps to lead him up to the main floor.

"Come back anytime, neighbor," Cindy said.

"You were right, John," he said. "This neighborhood is plenty accepting."

"The Vacation BBC Cure-All"

The forecast was bleak, and Trent emotionlessly sat upright in the concrete, angular hot tub off-center of the lagoon pool. There were only a few tourists nearby. Three ten-story buildings engulfed the guest recreation area, and none of the morning central Florida sun had yet to make its brief appearance.

Trent sighed and reclined his head back on the concrete and stared up at four of the blandest palm trees he'd ever seen surrounding the grotto and ticked off in his head the number of emails, phone calls, and instances of *bull*shit that were accruing at the office by the second whilst he "vacationed." Trent, by experience, could roughly average out each vacation day, necessitating twenty callbacks, fifty reply emails, and proofing a veritable ream of paperwork that required his eyes and execution.

He was dark-haired, lightly complected, and one of the "bosses" at the office, the cause of which no doubt contributed to the slow graying of what in his undergrad days had been the longest, silkiest rocker hair that was his magical co-ed pussy magnet. But those days were gone.

Most *days are gone*, he thought, feeling the familiar lump come up in his throat as his heart pulsated and then deliberately, via the "stop sign" mental exercise his therapist had taught him, he threw up red stop signs in all directions, the positive and the negative.

He had not yet mastered separating the mental grain from the chaff, so he shut down with no thoughts whatsoever, comfortable yet numb. He could not sleep, but listened to the swish-swish, swish-swish of the old timers hitting it early in the pool, before the storms were set to arrive.

"Fucking charter," he said as he thought of the nonrefundable fee he'd paid to at least get his line wet a few times to be able to say he had trophy fished. "*Fuck.*" He stewed, the sadness transitioning into anger and ultimately self-pity. He thought of the outstanding blood results awaiting him from the doc upon his return. *Please,* please, *let it be cancer,* he thought. *Just don't take my cock, Lord, anything but my cock.*

Regardless of the diagnosis, if any, he had no intention of treating, other than those the feelgoods the shrink prescribed him.

Eventually, Maria, also dark-haired but with resplendent skin from consistent tanning, emerged glowingly from the lobby of Building 12. Maria wore a turquoise sun hat, ornated around the brim with seashells Trent had purchased from a near-empty mall close to the beach the day prior.

She wore a one-piece black bathing suit and white bathrobe, open, showing her hourglass figure and ample breasts, but very little cleavage. Trent watched her saunter over to a set of cheap, white lounge recliners, put down her bag, disrobe, and then mosey over and down into the hot tub. She curled up beside him and kissed him on the cheek. Even with her Prada shades, he stared down at her through the lenses to her green eyes. She'd smiled ear-to-ear all the way to him.

"Good morning," she said, and squeezed him toward her.

"What's good about it?"

"We're here together. I'm so sorry about your trip. You know Florida—maybe this storm will pass through, and then you can call the company about going out. The weather disrupted our stay and our itinerary—I'm sorry."

He knew he shouldn't let it escalate, but the stop signs were slowly melting away in his mind, and the anger, fear, insecurity, and anxiety gave way to hurt. "I guess the weather found its way into the bedroom to throw off that itinerary."

She jolted back from him and held her ground: "I don't want to hear about it *anymore*. I can't help *nature*. I can't *help* my headaches. I can't help that even now that I'm off my period I just don't seem to do whatever it is you feel you need in the bedroom anymore. Do you want to go upstairs right now so you can ditch this fucking mood?"

Trent never backed down, to anybody. "Look, we agreed to branch out and do something adventurous or different and here we are having the usual sex we have and we're sitting in a hot tub like we have at home, as we do a pool, and if we were just going to sit around doing the same shit we do at home, we need to just back our bags and go home."

"Why? Why? So you can post up in your chair and 'not do work' while not relaxing at all?"

"Maria, I can relax better at home if we aren't going to go out. We were going to get an escort or go to the strip club. Something fun. Something different. You said you wanted to explore that side of yourself. I am so sick of this vanilla shit.

"I see what's up. I get to work at a job I fucking hate to provide for the family who rarely shows their gratitude and as an award, I get to sometimes have vanilla sex *if* we happen to get a 'sex window' *if* we get a sitter because you're neurotic when it comes to having sex with the kids in the house and here I am on a vacation where I wanted to break that mold a bit, and you're too chicken shit or tired or sick or whatever the *fuck* to get outside that box you like so much. We had a *deal*.

"I work my ass off all the time on *bullshit* to pay for a vacation, only to get down here and be fucking miserable because we're stuck in this dungeon you picked out—thank you—and *I am pissed*. At you. You made a promise, and you broke it and now I suppose it's time to just hunker down and be like my old man, coming home to kids that don't appreciate me and to a wife to have sex with maybe three times a month while she would rather cuddle and spoon than just fuck. You just can't lower those inhibitions just a little bit so I can feel like I'm a fucking human being from time to time, can you?"

"Those inhibitions, asshole, are because I love you. Is just a little intimacy too much to ask for from time to time or do you need some whore to grind her pussy against mine for awhile to make you happy?"

"I mean...*yeah*, that's a good start."

Maria pushed him again, this time with verve. "Why? Why do you want that? Why do you *need* that?"

"Because I need to decompress every now and again. Do you *not* understand the pressure I have?"

"Don't you do that. You know I do. I helped you get to where you are. I supported you through school! You don't get to blame the job. Walk away and get over this shitty darkness you've had that dictates the mood of the entire house. Walk away. We scraped by during school, but I stood by you then and--"

"No shit you stood by me!" He interrupted, to her dismay. "You know a good investment when you see one."

"Oh, fuck you, fuck you. You know I'm not that kind of woman."

She really wasn't, and Trent knew it, but he was out of fucks.

He doubled down: "Sorry, honey, I'll retract that, in part. I'll call your lifestyle and the kid's lifestyle a perk rather than an investment. Listen, I've had this week marked all damn year, and you're flaking, you fucking flaker. Do me a favor: I'm going to go on autopilot for the next twenty years. Flip the switch if you decide you want to broaden your horizons. Otherwise, I'll see you on the first, second, and fourth Thursdays of each month in the bedroom, contingent on a babysitter. If you want anything other than cuddling and spooning leading to brief, missionary sex where you cum in three minutes followed by going through the motions trying to rush me to cum just to get your 'matrimonial duties' over with, be sure to wake me up then too, 'k? Or hey, one more exception: When you and the kids decide I'm more than a walking wallet, I'd like to be awake for that, please."

Her lower lip quivered. "I'm sorry I'm not good enough for you anymore. I'm sorry you think any of that. We love you, *asshole*." Maria slunk out of the hot tub, the radiance long gone, and she walked slowly with her head down to her lounge chair. She reclined, pulled her hat down low, and crossed her arms. Her shoulders shook mildly every minute or two.

Trent sat in the abyss and decided to feel nothing again.

After about twenty minutes, Maria disappeared through the gate and around the bushes with her Marlboro Lights, cell, and lighter. Shortly thereafter, Trent detected that sweet stench of her cigarette in the picnic area. He hit his Miami Mint vape and could make out her sniffles, despite how low he knew she was trying to keep them at bay.

He vacated the hot tub and with malice aforethought took a lounge chair well behind the baker's dozen or so chairs that formed the section by the pool, where Maria had placed her belongings. Trent sat in the shade and resisted the urge to check his email. Instead, he looked at the page where he'd suggested a certain escort and Maria had agreed to meet with her. Despite his reminders, Maria had not given a single go-ahead on the plan as agreed to beforehand. He was done pushing. Point of fact, he was just *done*.

Some clouds had begun to form above just as a large, African American man emerged from Building 11 with nothing but his swim trunks, flip-flops, and towel on his shoulder. He was built and well-groomed, appearing to be in his upper forties, with a strong moustache. He towered over the scene, standing well over six-and-a-half feet. Methodically, he scanned the entirety of the pool area, saw the old timers gathered in the other areas off in the shade hee-hawing, and then Trent saw him set his eyes on Maria's section. He made a beeline that way, walking swiftly, deliberately.

"Ma'am," he said as he approached Maria, "do you know if any of these other seats are taken? Are you saving them for somebody?"

Maria wiped her nose and sniffled one last time. She looked up, a bit taken aback from how high he towered over her. "No, they're all free, but I appreciate you asking."

"Thank you, ma'am."

"You're more than welcome."

If he'd noticed Trent back behind the grove, Trent wasn't able to discern it. What he most definitely discerned was Maria tracing the gentleman with her eyes as he made his way to the lounge recliner at the exact opposite end of Maria, with four seats between them.

It was the hat turning that gave her away. The hat he'd seen at the mall that had reminded him of her. *Well, how about that shit?* he asked himself, dumbfounded by evolution and his wife concurrently.

He texted her:

Trent: I saw that.

Maria: What?

Trent: What do you mean "what"? I saw you literally eye-fuck that guy just now.

Maria: I most certainly did not.

Trent: Bullshit. You're welcome for the hat. You know, there's a way to move your eyes without moving your head.

Maria: Shit. SMH.

Maria: He was polite. That's it. My husband certainly isn't today.

Trent: You made a promise, and you broke it. I am now your husband-creditor.

Maria: Are you serious right now? We are having a shitty vacation, and I owe you a *debt* because of it?

Trent: You broke your contract. I'm entitled to damages. It's as plain and as simple as that.

Maria: Am I supposed to stop the weather?

Trent: No, but I can sure as shit pull up this text where you agreed we'd have five nights of intimacy and at least one wild sexual adventure we've never had before. You welched. You broke the contract.

Maria: You welched first.

Trent: Negative. I spooned you all night long and massaged your head with your headaches. I'm calling that intimacy. You're in default, chicken shit.

Trent looked up and saw Maria semi-collapse forward with frustration in her lounge chair.

Suddenly, she regained her composure and arose, scooting two chairs closer to the "polite" gentleman.

"I'm sorry, sir, I didn't catch your name."

He sat upright and stretched out to shake the hand she was offering. "I'm James. You?"

"Maria, it's very nice to meet you, James. Are you enjoying your stay here?"

"Oh, it's okay, I wish there were more clubs maybe, or someplace I could get out and socialize."

"Well, we're socializing right now, James," she said, and they both laughed. Trent saw it—that superficial visage she could enable at will from two decades of business socials at the company.

"Is your family with you?" Maria asked.

"Nah, I'm divorced. A few years now. I'm not going through that again."

"I can certainly understand your frustration," she said as Trent felt his blood pressure rise.

"Excuse me one second, James. I'm going to have a smoke," she said and began walking toward the smoking area.

"Yes, ma'am. I'm just glad to be talking to somebody," he said as he lounged back again, putting his hands behind his head, not a goddamn care in the world.

Maria buzzed him just as he smelled smoke again.

Maria: If you call me a chicken-shit again, I'm going to fuck that guy. If you want to see me get wild, I'll show you wild.

Trent: Yeahhhh, we spoke of having a threesome with a very female escort or hitting the VIP room at a strip club. I don't recall the phrase "gigantic black man presumably with a huge cock" anywhere in our conversations.

Maria: I'm sorry? So, who's the chicken shit now? I'm warning you: Don't you dare me. You want only what you want. If we agreed to have a vacation with wild adventures, and those adventures only involve your wants and needs, I have to wonder whether it's a valid contract.

Fuck, I should have never let her work for me, Trent thought to himself. Then again, in the good old days in his two-office shithole, she'd give him blowjobs at will when he got stressed, so, after running some quick calculations, Trent retracted his initial regret.

He thought of it for a moment—the notion of his wife, the woman whose body he knew as well as his own, who shared a common history intertwined with his, with many beautiful moments between them, getting plowed by James' presumed giant cock. Trent felt himself harden slightly, at the thought of it. He'd never seen her in that light. He thought of the pleasure she would experience with the entire length of James' cock inside her. Trent kept hardening for a moment and even sensed just a smidge of precum leak in his swink trunks.

Then, the rational part of his brain kicked back in. He knew she wouldn't do it. She didn't have the fucking balls. His negotiator instinct kicked in, and he knew this was an opportunity to make her feel worse, although he loved her. Still, he so desperately couldn't escape the darkness within himself enough to overcome his self-pity. He'd call her bluff, she'd back off, and that would be that. He'd have the higher ground again. Either he could drive all the way home just venting and bitching and letting it all out about how he fucking felt, or she'd cave on the escort.

Trent: I dare you to go back to your lounge chair, recline, and unclasp your bathing suit. Pull it down and let him see some of those big tits.

Maria: Watch this then.

Maria jump-scared Trent and even James snapped his head in the direction of Maria as she strutted through the entrance beside the hot tub lagoon, letting the gate slam loudly behind her. Her head was held high this time.

She sat uptight on the lounge chair and smiled at James flirtatiously as she unclasped her suit at the top of her neck. Trent caught James side-eye Maria, and Trent only then noticed how slick James was. He knew there were two kinds of guys when it came to checking out women: the "gawkers" who creeped women out, destined to be sad, old bastards filled with regret, and those who could hide their impure inquisitiveness, especially with the eyes. James was slick enough to look a woman up and down with the relative impact of a butterfly flapping its wings.

Maria pulled her straps down but held her hand open-palmed against her chest as she pivoted her feet onto the lounge chair and reclined with the straps down. She had pulled her top down just enough to reveal the untanned portion of the upper quarter of her breasts. A beautiful red and black dragon tattoo permeated its way from the midpoint of her left bicep, up onto her shoulder, and down her back.

Fuck, she's hot, he thought. There was a break in the clouds, and it made her skin glisten, the hues of her dragon pop. He thought of how enjoyable it was for him to slide his cock in between those massive breasts with large, round areolas, with a handful of lube or her spit.

He found himself caught in reminiscence when his phone vibrated, stirring him from his lurid yet sentimental memories.

Maria: What now?

Okay, she's just pulled her top down a little. That's all. There are a thousand women at the beach who do the same every day, he thought.

Fuck it.

James: Okay, now, honey, that granny twice your senior yonder across the pool is showing more tit than you. Pull it down lower.

She did as she was told and effortlessly slid down the top to point just above her nipples.
James' head turned ever so slightly in Maria's direction. She held her phone on her belly, screen up. She tapped the phone, and the taps echoed throughout the pool area.

Trent: *More.*

This time, however, she did not pull her top down further but turned over on her belly. She did not bother to secure her top or straps, so as she turned, she down-bloused Trent and James, revealing her erect nipples, just for a moment, until she lay supine. James' ability to not teeter on becoming a "gawker" was threatened when Maria, her bosom pressed downward on the chair, reached with both hands to the back of the bottom of her swimsuit. She pulled upward and inward, revealing wholly untanned areas, almost as if she were wearing a thong.

Trent: He's staring at your ass.

Maria: Good. I'm glad somebody appreciates it.

Trent: Let's see how much more he appreciates it. Turn on your right side and try to somehow stick your ass up in such a way that he can get a great view.

Dutifully, Maria turned to her right and feigned looking for an item in her bag at the back of the lounge chair. In doing so, she raised her curvy ass with cheeks with which you could grab just handfuls outward and upward.

It was then that he noticed both that he and James were hard. Trent's cock was so erect his blood pulsated. Trent's assumptions about Trent were true, and when Trent observed the massive, cylindrical erection in James' trunks, he wondered how the tip of his cock didn't stick out. James looked around while he stared at Trent's PAWG wife. Finding no apparent observers, James reached up into his trunks and gave the head of his cock a few tugs and squeezes, staring at Maria's big ass as she turned. This time, James gawked and Maria gawked right back at him, biting her lower lip.

Trent, in suit, began lightly stroking on himself, filled with both utter jealously yet complete arousal. His eyes darted back and forth between watching James admire Maria and then he would stare as Maria's ass. He knew had seen her ass at least twice a day for years, but this time, it was as if he were seeing her ass for the first time ever, through James, his proxy.

Trent: Do you like that he's hard as a rock right now looking at your ass?

Maria: I don't know. I'm unsure. I don't know how to feel right now.

Trent: Welll…I don't know. I don't know how to feel either. I know I'm hard as fuck too.

Maria: Are you serious?

Trent: Yep.

Maria: Mmmm. And he's hard right now, too?

Trent: He's about to explode.

Maria: Fuck, okay. Shit, is this okay? I'm getting wet and I don't know if I should be. Tell me what to do.

Trent: Well, okay, then, let me think.

Trent: I dare you to find some way to go sit next to him.

Maria: Okay. Here goes. Just stop me if you want me to stop this.

Trent: I just dared you.

Maria wrapped a towel around her waist and held up her top as she did what appeared to be a rather awkward scoot toward James.

"I'm sorry, but I haven't gotten to speak to anybody either, James, and the sun is just not hitting me right over there. May I sit down beside you?"

James, caught off-guard, tried to cover his gigantic penis with his towel, and fumbled it as he stuttered, "W-w-well, yes, ma'am. No problem."

"Why, thank you, James," she said as she navigated between her new seat and James and sat, loosely holding her top and blouse such that her breasts spilled out everywhere, and her side-boob grazed against James' shoulder.

"Oh my goodness, I'm so sorry for that. They pull these seats so close together."

"Oh you know these places, they'll squeeze a dollar out of a penny if they can."

Maria lounged, this time turning on her left side so her near-bare ass was facing Trent as her breasts, revealing everything but her nipples, were turned toward James. She cocked her elbow and rested her head against her palm.

Trent: Tell him you saw his hard-on.

"Speaking of squeezing something, James, there's no way you can hide what's underneath that towel right now, baby," Maria said as she stuck her ass out further in Trent's direction, who had already placed his towel on his own midsection.

"Oh, shit, I'm sorry about that. I saw the wedding ring, ma'am. I don't mean to be disrespectful. It's just...my body, you know." He emitted an awkward, apologetic laugh.

"Oh, don't you worry about that, James. Please call me 'Maria.' I find it very flattering. You're a very attractive man."

Trent knew James was smart enough by now to know James was seeing an opening. *Here we are*, he thought. *Here's the point she backs off. She'll never go there.*

Trent: Jerk him off underneath his towel.

Then, unlike all the previous texts, Maria simply glanced at her phone and then set it down within two seconds.

"Don't you worry about my husband. We've agreed to have a bit of a wild vacation with some freedoms we haven't given each other before, so you don't worry about that. Did I *actually* cause that?" she asked as she gestured toward his mid-section.

He started at her point-blankly: "Yes, you most certainly did, Maria."

"Well, hubby won't mind, and I can't imagine you're going to mind, so pull that towel a little further up and scoot closer." He quickly obliged, and Maria deftly slid her left hand discreetly under the towel and began stroking him, slowly and firmly.

"Oh, fuck, that's a giant cock. Fuck."

"Mmm, it's all because of you, baby, stroke on it faster."

Trent's stroking was in sync with his wife stroking James.

"Mmmm, baby, this is fuckin' hot. You've never felt this big of a cock before, have you?"

"No, baby, it's enormous. Fuck, I don't know where it starts or ends."

She stroked faster and faster, so fast that the effect of obscurity for which the towel was intended was rendered moot. Maria had slipped her right hand down, around, and into the bottom of her bathing suit, and Trent could tell she was fondling her clit. Trent felt himself literally on the verge of cumming in his shorts, where the amount of blood flow had caused Trent to notice that he had not been this hard in *years*. He could sense Maria's pleasure, and the thought of her pleasure made him even harder.

The old timers, having zero idea what was going on across the plaza, permitted James, Trent, and Maria to let themselves be pleasured or pleasure themselves relatively freely, in the moment together, and this continued until a family slammed the gate open to Trent's right near the hot tub. All three simultaneously did their best to cover and conceal their activities. What seemed to be ten different families rushed in, hopping into both the hot tub and pool, parents setting down their poolside gear in all sections, including where Maria and James had not four seconds earlier fooled around.

Maria, after clasping and affixing her clothing, grabbed her phone.

Maria: Well, what now?

Trent thought long and hard.

Trent: Get him up to our room. Take him to the apartment to the left in the suite. Leave the door barely open. Make sure the door to that apartment is positioned so I can see if you have the balls to suck his cock. You go with him. I'll wait five minutes and sneak in. Don't mention me.

Maria gathered her belongings, threw on her robe, and whispered something into James' ear. James nodded and accompanied her out of the pool area, guiding him by the hand, across the plaza, and into Building 12. The heavy steel door echoed as it slammed.

Trent sat up in his chair and set a timer. *Fucking deadlines even in Florida. Goddamn,* he thought, but those thoughts quickly turned to a mixture of lust, possessiveness, and naughty curiosity. *It's all bullshit,* he thought. *I'm going to find her up there by herself thinking this little display has proven her point.*

He watched the milliseconds, seconds, and minutes tick down to zero, each minute feeling like an eternity. He was so curious at that point about what was happening in Suite 10B of Building 12 that he felt nauseated. Did he want to find her sucking his cock? Or was this a marital power struggle? At what point should he back off? No, he couldn't. He wasn't the guy who backed off; he was the motherfucker from whom people backed away. He was a closer, a fixer. "ABC," baby.

No, fuck that, let her be the one to stop it. Let her be the chicken shit, and then she'd be sure to agree to bagging that nice petite blonde later. I'm not backing down, he thought.

Regardless, his finger hit the elevator button just as the timer went off. He'd lost some of his hardon, but it was becoming erect again from anticipation. Upon exiting the elevator onto his floor, he walked quickly but silently as he approached Suite A/B.

He exhaled and put his shaky hand on the handle, which

Maria had indeed left slightly ajar. He took off his flipflops, exhaled, and pushed through the exterior door and into the interconnecting lobby of the two apartments. The lights were out, shades pulled. He considered tiptoeing until it hit him that that was a futile effort. He did not hear slurping noises or the normal *mmm mmm mmm's* from her or James.

Quite the contrary: He heard Maria screaming in agonizing pleasure into a pillow. While he anticipated, at best, Maria giving a "Tuesday night hand job," as he fell into a sofa in the living room of apartment A, he saw his wife's face buried in a pillow with her ass up, James spanking her from behind as he ploughed her mercilessly.

She'd put the door back in an optimum position for him to watch her from the other suite without being seen in his dark corner. The rain had finally started falling and the darkness engulfed Trent as he pulled his trunks down, revealing a big, white cock.

Mine's not huge, he thought, *but it's fucking capable.*

Maria raised her head and noticed him through the angle of the mirror, and gave him just a slight, naughty smile before James grabbed her by the back of her dark hair and pulled her fully onto his cock. Trent could tell she was cumming just from the full size of James' cock penetrating her fully. She writhed, almost trying to crawl away from James to quiet the orgasm, but James was having none of that.

This time, he didn't pull her hair, but he pushed her face downward on the bed roughly and began fucking her with her in a prone position. James' muscular body was intimidating. Maria looked so soft and helpless, but her juices covered James' stomach, and Trent knew this wasn't about a deal anymore. She was taking that long black cock and loving every inch.

Trent stroked his cock, stifling his moans, trying not to cum. He was dizzy and confused, but he knew he loved her and loved knowing what pleasure she was experiencing at that point.

Trent licked some of his precum and used the remainder for lube. Suddenly, almost violently, James jerked Maria back into the doggie style position. Then Trent noticed it wasn't James fucking her, but rather Maria thrusting her hips back and forth on his cock, twerking, enjoying it all, giggling, moaning, cumming every few minutes. She was in the moment.

With James concentrating on fingering Maria's ass as she rocked back and forth with as much force as James had used on her, he did not catch Maria look up and mouth, "I love you, baby," to Trent and nodded her head, encouraging him to stroke that cock as she reached around and grabbed James' left hand, placing it on her left tit. Watching her tits bounce back and forth with each thrust, coupled with Maria's facial expressions he'd never seen before—it was as if she were grinding her teeth together and growling so she wouldn't explode—brought Trent to the brink of orgasm, but then he stopped himself.

He wanted her. *Badly*. His first thought was to simply pop in, but he elected to just watch, not stroking, but building his sexual energy as he watched her as she fucked James. From doggy, he tossed her on her back and fucked her missionary with her legs spread into a "V" and her hands squeezing his tight ass.

James then began teasing her. He took his cock out and circled its rim around her clit in a circle, sticking the head in every thirty seconds or so, just to torment her.

"No, no, no, no, no. Fuck me. Fuck me. *Fuck me!*" she begged.

"No," James said. "Let's see if you can deepthroat this cock."

Before Maria could even respond, James had knee-walked to the headboard and began slapping her face with his cock, each smack sounding like a baseball hit squarely. *Pop, pop, pop.*

"Your husband going to mind this?"

Maria fingered herself as she moaned each time James struck her with his cock. "Oh, he'd love it. He'd fucking love it. I don't know if he likes fucking me anymore, though."

"I'll make up for that, baby. Come on now, if you want more, you gotta earn it, wifey."

With that, the slapping subsided, and Maria began licking his balls and taint, rubbing his shaft as she licked his ass, balls, and then to his cock, where she tongued the rim of his cock ever so slightly, gripping and rubbing his balls.

Trent then saw Maria do something he'd never seen: She *spit* on James' black cock and began sucking on him with drool and James' precum dangling from both sides of her gaped mouth. Trent was again surprised when she didn't even do a test run. No, not Maria. She took what had to be ten inches of thick black cock, wider than a tallboy, and went right down on him to the fucking hilt. Over and over, she gagged but took it all. Periodically, she would stop to catch her breath, but James would thrust her mouth right back to the business.

Maria rose to her knees and pushed James back against the headboard so he could leisurely enjoy the blowjob.

"Oh fuck, wifey, you're so fucking good at that."

She stopped and teased him in return, tit-for-tat. "Call my 'Maria' if you want any more of this pussy." She lightly licked the head of his cock as she slid the tip of her index finger subtly into James' ass.

"Oh, god, oh fuck. I've never had that...what the fuck? Goddamn it. Please, it's too much. Let me cum in that pussy, Maria, please, baby, please. Awwww, *fuck*."

"Have you had the snip?" she asked.

"No, you?"

"No, but fuck it. I won't tell if you won't."

"I won't say anything. Please hop on this cock."

Maria then began fucking him reverse cowgirl, her big tits squeezed between her arms as she held her balance with her hands, riding James' cock, bouncing on it, flesh slapping against flesh. Both moaned with each downward motion by Maria. She increased her rhythm. Her dark was fluttered as she bounced on him rapidly.

"Fill this fucking pussy up, James," she said. "Fill me up before my husband gets back."

"Are you sure?"

"That wasn't a request, stud," she said. James held both her huge tits in his hands, and she fucked him faster and faster and faster until Trent heard James bellow: "Oh fuck, goddamn it," as he pulled Maria down so his seed would reach the furthest crevices of her pussy. James groaned as he spewed his spawn into Maria. Maria was climaxing again and kept jerking James' cock ever so slightly after he pulled out, methodically squeezing every drop of cum from him that she could. As she came, she held her arms upward and howled.

When she squeezed all his cum out, she rolled over, still cumming, still spasming. James, still mostly erect, mounted Maria and smacked his cock against her pussy, fiercely.

James repeated it, over and over, and then, for the first time, Maria squirted like a fire hydrant, covering James' sternum in her cum and some of his own. James then surprised Maria by ejecting one long final string of pearly white cum that shot from her landing strip to her face in a diagonal pattern.

Maria lay nearly lifeless. James relaxed beside her for a moment, but there was no cuddling. Maria was still experiencing aftershocks as James was pulling up his shorts.

"I'm sorry. That was hot, but when is your husband coming back? Do you know?"

"Oh, James," she said as she looked at him, glossy-eyed, "He's already here."

Trent saw James' eyes widen, and he took no time to verify the veracity of her statement, running out only in his swim trunks, calling back to her, "Hey, I'll see ya around maybe."

The door slammed behind him.

Both Trent and Maria remained silent in their respective apartments for a good five minutes, neither one quite comprehending what had just happened.

Eventually, Trent, weak-kneed, stood and pulled his clothes off. He stood at the doorway and saw Maria covered in cum, exhausted.

She turned her head to Trent. "You gonna reclaim this pussy or what, baby? Do you still want me?"

Trent approached the bed and stood at its foot. Maria's eyes were closed. James' cum leaked from her pussy, drip-drip-dripping. His encore money shot ran up her torso onto her face and hair.

Trent climbed onto the bed and on top of Maria. She looked up at him with those green eyes he had fallen in love with, and it was like the first time he'd *seen* her in *years*. He didn't know what to do. He didn't know how to feel other than what he felt—which was fiery lust and tender love.

With a nod from Maria, he entered her, and she gasped. She moaned sweetly, adoringly. She embraced him and stroked her fingertips lightly across his back. He made love to her slowly, deeply. He could distinguish James' cum from Maria's lovely nectar, and he grew harder, fucking her faster. This was *his* wife.

"Who does this pussy belong to?" he asked.

"You, baby. It's all yours. Forever."

He kissed her and, in doing so, inadvertently licked some of James' cum on her lower chin. Maria grabbed him by his hair and pushed him down on her left nipple, which was also saturated.

"Lick me clean, baby," she said.

He did what he was told and licked all of James' cum from her face, her tit, and stomach, and then the two made out together before Maria eventually swallowed it all. When he saw her gulp down all that thick cum from "Stranger James," he came, holding

Maria by the back of the neck, gently, pressing her against him.

Maria, queen for the day, felt how close Trent held her, embracing her, and with each shot into her, she kept teetering on the verge of orgasm until Trent began licking her right nipple like an ice cream cone and kept penetrating her despite his rapidly softening penis. She came once more. But this orgasm was different than that with James. They embraced each other as if they'd just bestowed their virginity on the other. It was a shared, singular, beautiful moment with rain falling and thunder rolling.

After what seemed like hours, Trent rolled off Maria. Both lay on their backs, breathing heavily, languidly.

"Well," Maria said, "Is my debt paid?"

"No more debts, baby. No more. I love you."

"I love you, baby."

And yet, somehow in that moment between Maria and Trent, the emergency cell went off on the bedside at full volume and rang as loud as a 1990s alarm clock.

Trent grabbed the phone.

"Yeah?" he asked Wendy, his paralegal.

"Sir, I'm sorry, but the partners have called an impromptu meeting to go over the budget and request your presence on vid cam. The junior associates are being lax about billing, and it's a whole thing, and I'm sorry to disturb you, but you know how they get, and they get mean when you're not here and—"

"Wendy, stop, stop, stop, stop. No, I'm not going to do that. Tell you what, do one last final thing for me, Wendy. Be my proxy. Tell the partners to add some new business to the agenda: If they're talking budgets, tell 'em I'm out and I want my cut. A man's gotta have his priorities. Later."

"Priorities?" Wendy asked, confused. "What fuckin' prio—"

Trent hung up, turned off both phones, and slept with Maria without a blanket, each wrapped in the natural warmth of the other.

ACKNOWLEDGEMENT

Moonbow Press wishes to acknowledge the very hard work that Kay has put into this work. Moonbow Press is dedicated to giving Southern authors a voice for their creative and non-fiction works.

NAUGHTY LACEY

Naughty Lacey is a series of novellettes and novels that will focus on everyday people in certain situations. The first Naughty Lacey series book (MATRIMONY) focused on marital situations. The second will focus on the relationship between fear and lust.

Fear

www.ingramcontent.com/pod-product-compliance
Lightning Source LLC
Chambersburg PA
CBHW051932240626
47153CB00004B/1464